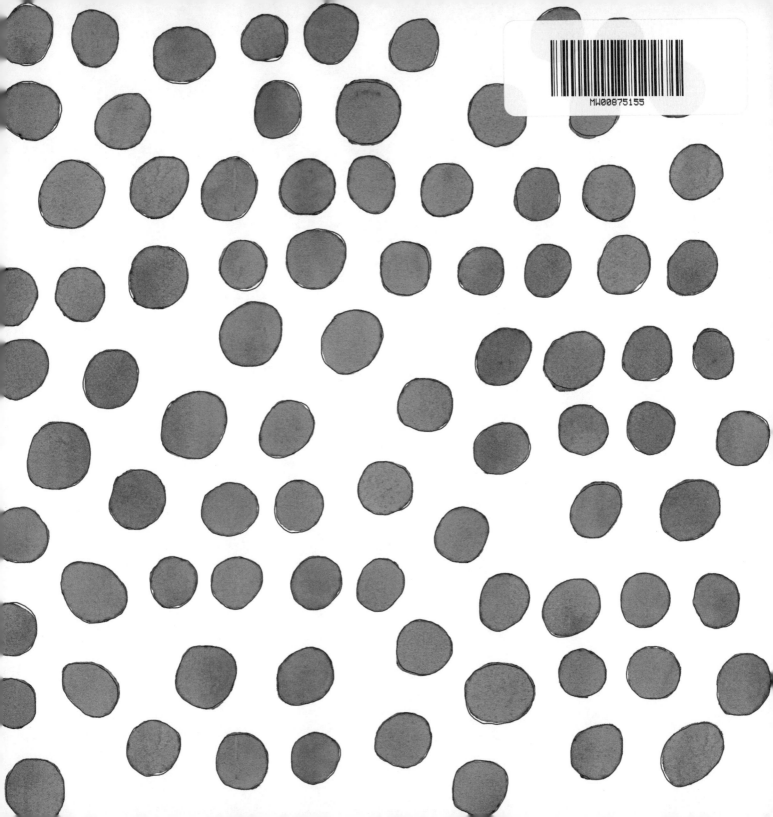

For Leo
-T.F.

For my Teeny Tiny
-K.L.

Special thanks to Paige Murray.

First Printing, 2016

Library of Congress Control Number: 2016907528
Tami Fitzkoff, Culver City, CA
ISBN-13: 978-0692702307 (Tami Fitzkoff)
ISBN-10: 069270230X

BE THE GRAPES

By Tami Fitzkoff

Illustrated by Kathlene Linehan

It was October,
and the neighborhood was humming.
Everyone was getting ready.
Halloween was coming!

I was eagerly anticipating going trick or treating

and getting my stomach ready for all the sugar I'd be eating.

There was a Halloween party
and everyone was invited.
I love candy and dressing up,
so I was very excited.

I needed to find a costume,
and Mom took me to the store.
There were funny glasses, scary masks,
spiders, and so much more.

I saw a bunch of kids grabbing costumes off the shelves—
superheroes, princesses, but not much else.

Then I saw the outfit that screamed out to me.

Big...

purple...

balloons—

that's what I wanted to be!

I asked my mom if I could wear it
for Halloween this year.
She smiled and said,
"That's funny! Of course you can my dear!"

I was ecstatic!
When I got home,
I immediately tried it on.
It made me feel so good that
I broke out into song.

I love my Halloween costume
and it doesn't need a cape! Oh, yeah!

It's super-duper awesome
and boy do I look grape! Oh, yeah!
Grapes! Get it?

I went to the party as happy as can be.
As soon as I got there, a kid walked up to me.

"What are you *wearing*?" he asked in a voice not so kind.
"I'm grapes!"
He looked at me like I was out of my mind.
"You know, grapes. The fruit. You eat it. The food."
He said, "That's a really *stupid* costume, dude!"

I walked over to the corner
then sat down and cried.
My mother came over.
She saw I was trying to hide.

"What's the matter, baby?" she asked and then kissed my head.
"My costume stinks! I should have worn a different one instead."

She said, "Look around the room, my dear. Tell me what you see."
"I see a lot of kids having fun...but not me."

"Well," she said, "I see a whole lot
of costumes that are exactly the same.

"There are ten Action Harries and ten Princess What's-her-names.

"No one else is quite as original or made a choice so neat.
No one else makes me prouder. No one else is quite as sweet.
Being different and unique is special, don't you agree?
If everyone were the same, how boring would that be?

"Now pick your head up,
and don't let anyone stand in your way.
Remember how much you loved this
costume yesterday?"

My mom made me feel better, so I got up and joined the crowd.
And before I knew it, I was having fun and laughing right out loud.

It turned into a great time, even though it started out quite tragic.
But with a little help, and some special words, things can change like magic.

Never be afraid to be yourself, no matter what people say.
It's your life to live, and you can do it your way.

People will hurt your feelings, like bruises, cuts, and scrapes,
but don't let them change you. Go on out there and...

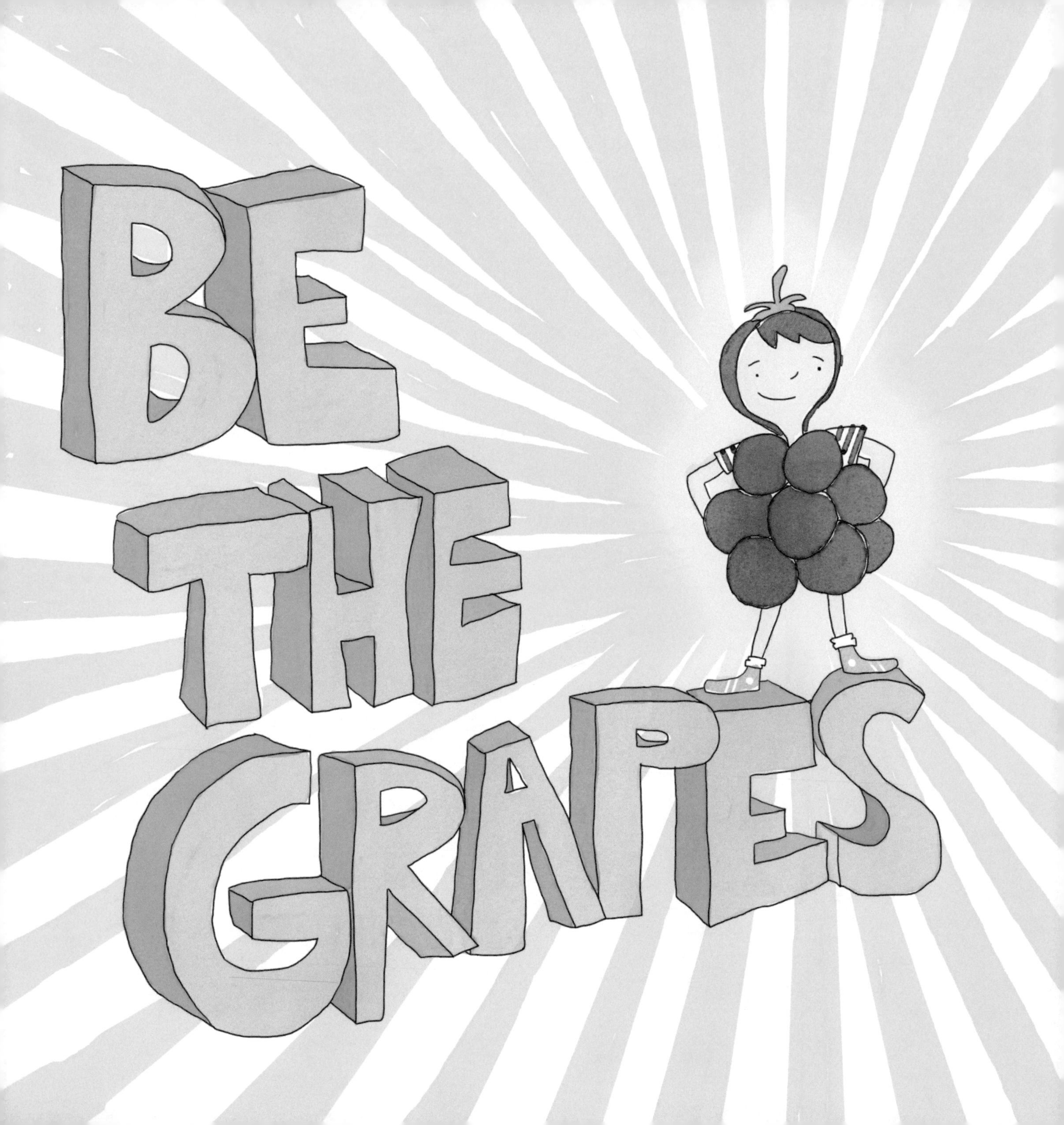
BE THE GRAPES

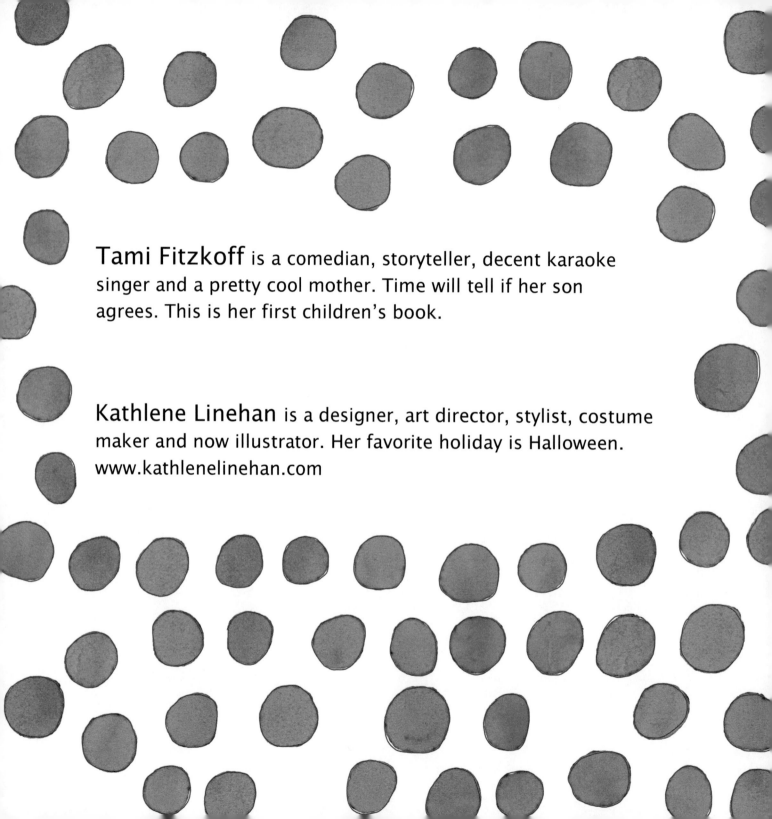

Tami Fitzkoff is a comedian, storyteller, decent karaoke singer and a pretty cool mother. Time will tell if her son agrees. This is her first children's book.

Kathlene Linehan is a designer, art director, stylist, costume maker and now illustrator. Her favorite holiday is Halloween. www.kathlenelinehan.com

Made in the USA
Middletown, DE
27 August 2016